Connect is published by Stone Arch Books
A Capstone Imprint
1710 Roe Crest Drive
North Mankato, Minnesota 56003
www.capstonepub.com

Library of Congress Cataloging-in-Publication Data
Cataloging-in-publication information is on file with the Library of Congress.
ISBN 978-1-4965-2585-7 (library binding)
ISBN 978-1-4965-2682-3 (paperback)
ISBN 978-1-4965-2679-3 (eBook PDF)

Editor: Jennifer Huston
Designer: Veronica Scott

Cover illustration:
Tony Foti

Printed in the United States of America in
North Mankato, MN.   009221CGS16

CONNECT

TOMMY MCKNIGHT
AND THE
GREAT ELECTION

by Danny Kravitz

STONE ARCH BOOKS
a capstone imprint

CHAPTER 1

NO MORE HAPPY DAYS

Crack! The ball shot off my bat and went sailing over a car. It bounced off the sidewalk and came to a stop on the side of the street. Kids chased after it as I ran to the fire hydrant that we used for first base. "Run, Tommy! Run!" my teammates yelled. I sprinted faster and faster. Soon I was running so fast that I lifted into the air and flew across the sky. Whoa! And then I saw FDR, Franklin Delano Roosevelt, the governor of New York. What's he doing here? And who are all these people with him? And what's that song they're singing? "Happy days are here again, the skies above are clear again ..."

And then I woke up.

I looked around my room. The sky above me was the yellow, water-stained ceiling, and I realized that I was dreaming. I must have dozed off after coming up to my bedroom after school.

"Happy days are here again," I heard someone singing along with the radio in the apartment next door. It was the theme song for FDR's campaign for president. It seemed like it was always on the radio.

I looked out the window of the small apartment where I lived with my parents. We lived on the top floor of a three-story building in Brooklyn. On the street some neighborhood boys were playing stickball. It was early fall and the leaves were just starting to change colors to golden yellow, blazing orange, and crimson red. The air was warm, and it felt sticky on my face.

I watched as one boy pitched the ball to the batter, who swung his stick and smacked the ball over the heads of his friends. The boy playing shortstop leaped to make the catch. It grazed his fingertips and then hit the ground nearby, so he went chasing after it.

"Hurry, George!" some kids yelled to the boy running after the ball. The ball came to a stop under a junky old Model T. The car was rusty and missing two of its wheels. George ran over, crawled under the car, and quickly emerged. "Quick! Throw the ball to Stanley!" the pitcher cried out. George threw a perfect strike from the car all the way to the tree the boys were using as third base. The third baseman's tag just barely missed the runner, Wally Strickler.

"Look at that, fellas," said Wally, "another triple. The Yankees will be calling me soon." Wally was a big, strong kid with a mop of brown hair. He was panting from his trip around the bases. He could sure whack a ball, but he wasn't very nice.

I gazed down at the rusty old Model T again, and then looked at the metal braces on my legs. They were held in place by thick brown leather straps that stretched around my thighs. They rubbed on my skin whenever I moved and left red marks and blisters. I looked back at the kids playing outside and realized that even though I wanted to be like them—hitting and running and throwing—I felt more like that broken-down car. Since I had polio about a year ago, my legs haven't worked right. I haven't been able to run or jump or play stickball. Not with those metal things around my legs—legs that won't move like they used to. I have enough trouble just walking with the crutches I use to help balance myself.

So there I was. It was the fall of 1932, and instead of playing stickball like other 12-year-old boys, I was stuck inside. Some luck I was having.

And there it was on the radio again. "Happy days are here again." Well not for me. Happy days were for other people.

I wasn't going to sit around in my room any longer. I grabbed my crutches, left the apartment, and soon I was hobbling down the stairs.

I got maybe three steps out the front door when Wally and his big mouth started teasing me. "Hey Polio Legs! How's them polio legs of yours?"

They aren't polio legs, ya dumbbell, I thought to myself. *They're my legs. I just happen to have had polio, a viral disease that affected my nerves and muscles. That's why my legs don't work right.*

I glared at Wally, but I didn't say anything. He wouldn't understand it anyway. He wouldn't understand anything other than what a great stickball player he was. I did my best to ignore him and just kept going.

I was a little embarrassed walking down the street with my braces and crutches. There were always tons of people out, and I felt like they were all looking at me. I knew I was probably wrong. They had their own problems to worry about. The stock market had crashed three years ago, and since then, a lot of people had lost their jobs. Some had lost their homes too. Many people didn't have enough money for food or clothes. They probably didn't even notice me, but it sure *felt* like they were staring as I walked by.

Well, it's still better to be outside, I thought. *It's better than being cooped up in my room.* Besides, I couldn't just sit around the apartment feeling sorry for myself. My family was going through a tough time like everyone else in the neighborhood. But I didn't notice it too much. What I *did* notice was that I couldn't walk right … and that Wally called me Polio Legs.

Thing is, I did have someplace to be. I just wasn't in any hurry to get there. I had a physical therapy appointment at the hospital, and I wasn't looking forward to it at all.

CHAPTER 2

THE "PAIN IN THE RUMP" ROOM

When I got to the hospital, a bunch of people were standing outside handing out fliers that said, "ELECT FDR." They were chanting, "In Hoover we trusted, now we are busted! In Hoover we trusted, now we are busted!" The presidential election was less than two months away, and it was a big deal to a lot of people. It seemed like every afternoon there was something going on, like a rally or a speech. Some people liked the current president, Herbert Hoover. But many blamed him for the Great Depression. It seemed like more and more people in New York wanted FDR to become our new president.

One of the chanters caught my eye—the mother of Beverly Braintree, a girl at my school who was just the prettiest girl I'd ever seen. But thank goodness Beverly wasn't around because I didn't want her to see me galumphing along on my crutches.

Oh no! There she was. I hoped she didn't see me. I kept my eye on her as I did my best to hurry behind the crowd toward the back of the hospital. Beverly was wearing a rosy pink ribbon in her copper-colored hair as she handed out fliers.

I don't really know why I liked Beverly so much. I just knew that I felt happy when I was around her. And when she looked at me with her sweet smile, I got little goose bumps on my arms. I liked talking to her too. At least I used to before I had to start wearing these stupid braces on my legs. There were a lot of things I liked to do before I came down with polio, like playing stickball and swimming. Even talking to girls like Beverly.

I watched as she turned to chat with her mother. Her baby blue dress had pale pink flowers on it, and it seemed to shine in the sun. I tried to pick up my pace, but an older boy startled me when he shoved a flier at me. "In Hoover we trusted, now we are busted!" he shouted. "Make sure your parents vote that bum Hoover out of office," he said. Couldn't he see that I didn't give a hoot about Hoover? I just wanted to get away before Beverly saw me. I wanted to get to the back entrance of the hospital before …

"Hey Tommy!" Beverly called out. Oh no! She saw me. Just my luck. My heart did a flip-flop in my chest at the sound of her voice. Unable to think straight, I smiled sheepishly, gave her a slight wave, and kept plodding on.

As I turned the corner near the back entrance of the hospital, my crutch hit a banana peel and I went sailing through the air. A banana peel? Come on!

When my crutches went flying, I crashed to the ground, and my face smacked the concrete. I could handle a little pain, but I had ripped a hole in the knee of my new trousers … the ones that Mom had just made so I could have a nice pair of pants. Ugh! What a day!

I crawled across the alley to retrieve my crutches, then pulled myself back to my feet. *I don't even want to be here for physical therapy*, I thought. The physical therapy was supposed to make my legs stronger. The truth was, I wanted the polio to go away the same way it came: I wake up tomorrow, and it's gone.

It all happened so fast. Last summer I went to visit my grandmother in western New York. I had so much fun swimming in the lake every day with the kids that lived there. A few days after I got home from Grandma's, I started feeling really tired and achy. I was shivering, even after taking a hot bath. When I woke up the next morning, I just didn't feel right. And my back was stiff. Then my legs started to feel stiff too. And they hurt. Over the next few days, it got worse. Before I knew it, the doctor was at our house saying things like, "I'd like to talk to you about polio," and "There's no cure for polio." Mom was crying, and I was thinking, *What's happening? What is polio?* Turns out, polio was me now. One week I was swimming, the next week I couldn't even walk.

I made my way through the hospital into the large room they called the PT room, or PTR. PT stands for physical therapy, which is all about doing exercises that help your body get stronger. I liked to say that PTR stands for "pain in the rump" because, for me, doing physical therapy was about as much fun as having a toothache. But I had to admit that there was one reason why it wasn't so bad. Or I should say, one person: Ruby.

Ruby was my physical therapy nurse. And she was the only good thing about having polio. She was Haitian, meaning she moved here from the island of

Haiti. She had dark skin, shiny black hair, and a smile so bright that it lit up the room.

When I arrived, Ruby was standing there with her big, strong hands on her hips. "There's my strong mon. Come in, come in, ya silly one," she said with that beaming smile.

She talked sort of funny. Her words bounced back and forth like a yo-yo on a string. "Ya lookin' strong … so strong," Ruby said. "Get on in here, my strong one, so we can make ya stronger."

With Ruby I did all kinds of exercises. I moved my legs up and down, pushed against her hands with my feet, and tried to walk without my braces or crutches. It was hard work, but Ruby made it seem fun.

Today, she had me lie on my side and lift my legs one at a time. "Lift now, Thomas," she said encouragingly.

So I lifted … or tried to anyway. I only got my foot about an inch or two off the table before my leg plopped down with a thud. "Again," Ruby instructed. So I lifted again.

"Higher now," she said. I lifted and lifted but … WOWZER! It was hard work! My leg slammed into the table. "Good job! That's better than last week," she said.

Ruby had explained that I may have gotten polio from swimming in the lake. She said that lots of people get it, but it only causes muscle problems in a small group of people. Just my luck!

"How is this supposed to help?" I asked Ruby.

"Well, for one thing, you are retraining your muscles to do things the way they used to," she answered. "I can tell you're getting stronger."

"What's the second thing?" I inquired.

"The second thing is that I'm working my magic on you, and you have to believe."

"Seriously?"

"Seriously, my boy. If you don't believe, you shan't receive."

"Swell ..." I replied with a note of sarcasm.

"Do you believe, Thomas?"

"That I'll get better?"

"Yes."

Truthfully, I didn't know. I mean, polio hit me like a water balloon that I never saw coming. And once I was wet, I couldn't get dry. It was just so strange to have my legs not work. They said I might regain some muscle strength, but I wasn't so sure.

The thing I liked most about working with Ruby is that we always spoke honestly. So I told her the truth, "I'm not sure."

She gave me that all-knowing look of hers and then another big smile lit up her face. "We'll work on that later," she said. "For now, let's work on you lifting your legs some more. You ready?"

What else was there to do?

When I left the hospital, it was my favorite time of day, so I was in no hurry to get home. It was just starting to get dark. The streets were quieting down, and it was very peaceful.

But when I got to my building, Wally and his buddies were hanging around. I tried to reach my apartment door without them seeing me, but I couldn't move fast enough. As I got to my stoop, I heard, "Hey, Polio Legs! Catch!" I turned to see a ball sailing right at me. Instinctively, I reached up to block the ball from hitting me, but it was too late. It nailed me right in the chest and knocked the wind out of me. I fell over … again!

Wally burst out laughing. "Did you see that, boys? Did you see how Tommy just fell over?"

I'd had enough of Wally. I picked up the ball and struggled to get back up with my crutches.

"That was funny," Wally said.

"You know what, Wally," I said. "If we were friends and I was in on the joke, it might have been funny. But we're not friends, so it was just mean." I threw the ball on the ground.

"So what are you gonna do about it?" Wally teased.

That was actually a very good question, considering my situation. "I'm going to go upstairs and have a laugh thinking about how stupid you are, Wally," I said.

That got a chuckle … not from Wally, of course, but from the other kids. It must have really made Wally mad because he let out a grunt and lunged toward me. Uh-oh!

I quickly headed for the door, and just before he could get to me, I got inside and slammed it shut. I began making my way up the three flights of stairs, but I wasn't laughing. Getting hit with the ball and being made fun of really hurt. And being mean to Wally didn't make me feel any better. In fact, before I opened the door to our apartment, I had to wipe away a tear that was running down my cheek.

CHAPTER 3

TO RUN OR NOT TO RUN

The next morning before school, I went with my mother to get some free bread. We waited in a breadline with others. For many people without jobs or with little money, it was the only way they could afford bread. It was the same for us.

After that I walked to school with my buddies, Nicky and Boris. Nicky and I had been friends since we were babies because our mothers were friends. His grandparents came here from Italy a long time ago. All the girls had a crush on Nicky because of his wavy black hair and his brown, puppy-dog eyes. Nicky was the best stickball player among us, but he also loved drawing and making things with his hands. Before I got polio, I loved to play stickball too.

We met Boris five years ago when his family moved into the neighborhood after leaving Russia.

They had escaped something called religious persecution, where people were attacked simply for being Jewish. It was kind of like Wally bullying me because of my legs, only much worse. When Nicky and I met Boris at school, we loved his sense of humor, and we all became friends.

Every day Nicky and I met Boris in front of his parents' grocery store. He was waiting for us on top of a horse-drawn wagon full of food that was being unloaded.

Once we got to school, I saw a big sign in the hallway that said, "Run for Student Government." I was looking at the sign, remembering how I'd wanted to run for student government before I got polio. Just then I felt a tap on my shoulder. It was Beverly.

"Hi Tommy," she said. She was wearing a sunny yellow dress with a matching ribbon in her hair. "You thinking of running for student government?"

"Oh, um, no," I said as I turned my back to the sign, pretending I hadn't been looking at it.

"Well, the elections are coming up. Speaking of which, I saw you at the rally for FDR yesterday. You left so quickly that I didn't get to say hello."

"I, uh, I was late for an appointment," I said.

"Oh, yeah. How's your physical therapy going?"

"Just great," I said. "I don't plan on having these things for much longer," I fibbed, waving one crutch in the air as I leaned on the other for support.

"You're so brave, Tommy!"

Brave? I thought to myself. *How am I brave?*

"And I think you're going to be just fine. You know, you really should run for student government. You'd be great at it."

I knew a little about student government. The members organized school events like dances and fund-raisers. They also created clubs like the chess club and math club. You could be president, vice president, treasurer, or secretary. It was a lot like the real government, which I'd been interested in ever since we learned about the American Revolution and the founding of the United States in history class.

"I hadn't really given it much thought," I fibbed again.

"Well maybe you should. See you later, Tommy," she said as she walked off. As I watched her go down the hall, I felt butterflies in my stomach, and I couldn't stop thinking about her smile.

I went over to the drinking fountain to get some water. Just as I started to feel the cold water on my lips, someone pushed my head into the fountain.

My face was covered with water as I turned around to see Wally standing there. "Hey, Polio Legs!" he said.

I shouldn't have been surprised, but I just couldn't believe it. Some kids were laughing at me, which made me embarrassed. I could feel my face turning red, but I'm not sure if it was from embarrassment or the anger boiling inside me. If I didn't need those stupid crutches to stand on my own, I would have punched Wally right in the face. But I wouldn't do that. And that made me just as angry as Wally's bullying.

At dinner that night, my parents talked about the upcoming presidential election. According to Pop, FDR had better ideas for getting the country out of the Depression than Hoover did.

"How's dinner, boys?" Mom asked.

"Dinner is delicious, sweetheart," Dad said. Dad had lost his job as a bookkeeper and now only worked here and there doing odd jobs. He was frustrated about not having money, but he tried not to let it show.

Dinner was ham, potatoes, and dandelion salad. It tasted fine, but sometimes lately, I didn't have much of an appetite.

"Not hungry, Thomas?" Mom said.

"Nah. It tastes good, though."

"I hope you're not coming down with something," she said, as she placed her hand on my forehead.

"No, I'm fine … just not that hungry," I said.

"OK," she said, sounding a bit concerned. "By the way, I sewed up that hole in your pants. They're as good as new."

"Thanks, Mom," I said. "Sorry that I tore a hole in them."

Pop showed me an article in the newspaper about FDR coming to give a couple of speeches in New York. "Would you like to go?" he asked.

"Sure, Pop," I said. But I didn't really care one way or the other. "Can I be excused?"

"You may, son," Pop said.

"I'll put your dinner in the icebox in case you get hungry later," Mom said. As I got up from the table, I saw Mom and Pop exchange a look. I could tell they were worried about me.

In my room, I sat on my bed trying to decide if I should run for student government. I also thought about Beverly and how I had liked talking to her at school today. I sat up and looked out my bedroom window. Then I saw that broken-down Model T, sitting there all alone. It reminded me of how sad and lonely and helpless I felt.

CHAPTER 4

FDR AND ME

A few days later, I was coming back from physical therapy when I passed two men talking on the sidewalk. One of them pointed at me and said, "Do you really want *that* for president?"

I turned and looked at him. He had an angry look on his face under his wool cap, and his hands were rough and dirty. "What did you mean by that, mister?" I asked.

His friend smiled at me and gave him a playful shove. "Yeah, what did you mean by that, ya dumb palooka?"

"Me?" he asked in surprise.

"Yes, you, sir. I've heard my share of insults, but I don't even *understand* this one," I said.

"Oh, I'm really sorry, kid. I didn't think you could hear me. I wasn't making fun of ya. Really, I wasn't."

"So what did you mean?" I asked again.

"I was talking about Roosevelt. There's a lotta people out of work. But what does he care? He's a rich guy. We've all heard those promises before. We need a president who will get people back to work."

"Aw, he don't need your whole sob story, Paulie," said the other guy, whose name turned out to be Ralph. "You're just lucky the kid didn't take his crutch and give you a nice whack in the shin for having a big mouth." Ralph smiled at me and kicked Paulie in the shin.

"Hey! Cut it out!" Paulie grumbled. "I'm in a bad mood with all this election stuff. I'm outta work, and I just don't think that Roosevelt is the right guy for the job. Sorry for my loud mouth, kid."

"But what does that have to do with me?" I asked again, still confused. "Why did you point to me and say, 'Do you want *that* for president?'"

"Oh, because Roosevelt had polio."

"Huh?" I said, puzzled by what I was hearing.

"Yeah, just like you. He gets around on crutches ... even uses a wheelchair sometimes."

"FDR had polio?" I couldn't believe it.

"Oh, yeah. Got it about 10 years ago," Ralph explained. "And as far as I'm concerned, he's a better man for having it. So don't let it stop ya, kid."

But I was no longer listening to Paulie or Ralph. *FDR had polio.* I thought to myself as I started home. *Wow! And he's running for president. How's he doing that?* This was very interesting ... very interesting, indeed!

"Sure, FDR had polio," Pop said. We had just sat down for dinner.

"Do people know?" I asked.

"Sure they do. They just don't make a big deal about it," Mom said.

"Because it *isn't* a big deal," Pop added. "Listen, FDR might have had polio, but he's not going to let it stop him from doing anything."

"But don't people mind?"

"Nope," said Pop.

"That man on the street minded."

"There's always going to be somebody who thinks silly things," Pop said.

"Do you think he's embarrassed about it?"

"No. I'm sure there are moments when he feels awkward. But not often enough to stop him. In fact, FDR went to the Democratic National Convention *in person* to accept his nomination for president. No one else has ever done that before, so clearly he has nothing to hide."

Wow! This was incredible news!

"Most people just don't make a big deal out of it," Mom chimed in. "And you know why, dear?"

"Why?" I asked.

"Because *FDR* doesn't make a big deal out of it," Mom answered.

"Because it's not a big deal," Pop said again.

Roosevelt had polio, I thought to myself. *And he might become president!*

I had my doubts about whether or not it was a big deal to Roosevelt or if he felt embarrassed. But for the first time in a long time, I didn't feel so sorry for myself. In fact, I felt pretty excited.

CHAPTER 5

WHAT HAVE I GOTTEN MYSELF INTO?

Crack! The ball shot off my bat and went sailing over a Model T. The ball soared over a tree, bounced off the ground, and rolled down the sidewalk. Kids chased after it as I ran to the fire hydrant that was first base. "Go, Tommy! Go!" they screamed. Faster and faster I sprinted. And as I ran, I saw a bright, bright light ...

I woke to the sun shining in through my window. It was early on Saturday morning. I got dressed and went outside to find Nicky.

"Nicky, did you know FDR had polio?" I said as I approached him sitting on the stoop of his apartment building. He was whittling a piece of wood with a knife.

"No," he said. "I didn't know that."

"What's that?" I asked, pointing to the wood.

"Oh, this is the Statue of Liberty." It looked like a stick of butter with a smiling face scratched into it.

"So, can you believe FDR had polio?"

"Wow," said Nicky. "And he's going to be president! At least that's what my ma says."

"I know," I said, hardly able to contain my excitement. "I know!"

After talking about FDR with Nicky, I realized that I really wanted to be in student government. *And I'd be good at it too,* I thought. I liked working with people and I wanted to do good things for our school. So why shouldn't I run? I mean, if FDR can run for president with polio, why couldn't I be on the student council with braces on my legs? I was excited to do it *before* I got sick, so why let polio stop me? Monday was the last day to sign up. So come Monday morning, that's exactly what I would do.

At school Monday morning I saw Beverly in the hall. "Hi Beverly," I said. "I wanted to let you know that I've decided to run for student government."

"That's great, Tommy!" she said with a smile. "I told you you'd be great. And, of course, I'll vote for you. I'll even help you write your speech if you want."

"Speech?" I said. "What speech?"

"You know you're going to have to give a speech. We can talk about that later. I have to get to class," Beverly said.

I just stood there stunned as she walked away. How could I not know that I'd have to give a speech? I felt sick to my stomach just thinking about speaking in front of a bunch of people. What had I gotten myself into?

"Who will I have to give the speech to?" I asked Boris and Nicky. It was lunchtime, but I couldn't eat. I was so nervous just thinking about giving a speech that I felt like I had a big rock in my stomach.

"A lotta people ... the whole school, I think," Boris said, as he took a bite of his peanut butter and jelly sandwich.

"The *whole entire* school?" I asked. I was starting to panic.

"Don't you remember listening to the speeches last year?" Nicky asked.

"I guess I must have missed school that day," I replied.

"Don't worry … you'll be great," Boris said as he took another bite of his sandwich.

Would I be great? I thought to myself. *Sure. Why not? What's the worst that could happen?* I'd have to stand on the stage in front of everyone. And the kids might laugh at my braces and crutches. That seemed pretty bad.

"Don't worry about your crutches," Nicky said, as if he'd read my mind. "But first you have to get on the ballot. You should do it now."

"OK, OK," I grumbled.

I walked across the lunchroom to the student government sign-up table. I could feel beads of sweat forming on my forehead. Not only was I nervous about signing up, I was even nervous about people *seeing* me sign up.

No one is watching, I reassured myself. *No one cares.* I took a breath and moved toward the table. When I got there, the boy at the table said, "Would you like to sign up for student government?"

"I would."

"Great. Sign here," he said as he handed me a pencil.

I started to sign my name, but I was so nervous that I pushed too hard, and the pencil tip broke off. "Uh … sorry. Do you have another pencil?" I asked.

He chuckled and said, "sure," as he handed me the pencil from behind his ear. "Sign here, then take this paper and get 50 signatures. Once you get 50 signatures, you'll be placed on the ballot."

"Um, uh … 50?" I stammered.

"Yep, 50. But don't worry. It's not as hard as it sounds."

"OK. If you say so," I mumbled.

As I turned to walk back to Nicky and Boris, I passed a group of guys from the chess club. They stood up and clapped and shouted, "Well done, Tommy! Good for you!"

So much for nobody noticing me. Now everyone stopped to take a look. And more people started cheering, which brought more attention to me.

I could feel a warm sensation come over me as my face turned beet red. I wanted to run away, but that was impossible. Then I saw Beverly smile at me. Before I knew it, nearly everyone in the lunchroom was clapping and cheering me on.

And then I did something unexpected. I mean, I did it, but it was like I was watching myself do it. I raised my right arm up—crutch and all—then swooped it across my body and took a bow.

Well, that seemed like a pretty good time to start getting signatures, so I headed over to the chess club guys. The six of them were my first signatures—my very first supporters.

CHAPTER 6

THE CAMPAIGN BEGINS

The rest of the day, I felt a sense of purpose. I had until Friday to get my signatures, but I also had to decide which office I would run for. Would it be president? Vice president? Treasurer? Because this was my first campaign, I wanted to learn more about FDR and politics in general.

Before heading home, I stopped by the school library. I asked the librarian, Mrs. Lambeeny, to help me find me some information on FDR.

"Writing a report, are you?" she asked.

"No, ma'am. I've decided to run for student council."

Mrs. Lambeeny looked down at me and smiled. "I bet you'll be an excellent candidate, Thomas." Then she was off. A moment later—BAM!—a stack of books, magazines, and newspapers landed on the table in front of me.

I sat down and started reading. Turns out Roosevelt got started in politics as a state senator in 1911. Then he ran for vice president in 1920.

But then one of the magazine articles caught my eye. There was a picture of FDR swimming in a lake or a pond. The headline read, "FDR REHABS POLIO AT WARM SPRINGS." *What was that all about?* I wondered. *Was he getting better because of the water?* I couldn't wait to find out.

"Why was he in the water?" I asked Ruby later during my physical therapy session.

Ruby explained that Roosevelt was doing his physical therapy exercises in the waters of Warm Springs, Georgia. In the water he could move in ways that he couldn't on land. It helped him strengthen his weakened muscles.

"Then that's what I want to do," I told Ruby. "What do you think?"

"I don't swim," she said.

"What do you mean you don't swim?"

"I mean I don't swim … I'm afraid of the water."

"But you grew up on an island!"

"Not everything makes sense, Thomas," Ruby replied.

"But how are you going to help me do my exercises in the water if you're afraid of the water?"

"Hmmm ... That's a good question." Ruby looked at me for a moment and then broke into her big smile. "But we'll figure it out, my strong mon."

Coming up the stairs to the apartment, I was hit by the tasty smell of baked potatoes and butter. And if I wasn't mistaken, I smelled chicken soup. We barely got meat these days now that Pop wasn't working much.

As we sat down for supper, I asked my father, "Pop, if Roosevelt gets elected, do you think he'll create more jobs for people?"

He looked at me with a curious grin. I could tell he enjoyed these conversations. "It's hard to know for sure until he's in office," Pop replied.

I took a big gulp of my chicken soup. It was amazing how the chicken made it taste so much better than when Mom could only afford to use water, potatoes, and a few carrots. "So, what's the difference between FDR and Hoover?" I asked.

My father leaned back in his chair and scratched his chin. "Well one thing Hoover believes is that the government should help banks and businesses in order to improve the economy."

"What about FDR?" I asked.

That's when Mom spoke up. She read a lot—books, magazines, and the newspaper. "FDR wants the government to create jobs and make prices and wages fair for everyone. That will help boost the economy and restore peoples' confidence in it."

"Because if they have confidence that things are getting better, they're more likely to spend their money?" I asked.

"Exactly! Very good, son," said my father.

"How did you learn what the candidates want to do?" I asked.

"Well, they give speeches," Pop replied. "In FDR's nomination acceptance speech, he talked about all of this."

FDR has to give speeches, just like I do. "I'd like to read that," I said.

"What's with the sudden interest in the election, Thomas?" Pop asked.

"I've decided to run for student government at school," I answered.

"Oh, that's wonderful, dear!" my mother exclaimed. "How about some more soup?" I nodded as she picked up my empty bowl.

"Oh and guess what I found out? FDR uses water and swimming as part of his physical therapy. And Ruby said we might be able to do that too," I said excitedly.

"Sounds like you've had a productive day," Pop said.

"What office are you going to run for?" Mom asked.

I smiled proudly and sat up straight, puffing out my chest a little. "President," I said. "Just like FDR."

At lunchtime the next day, I started getting more signatures. Most people were happy to sign my paper. Maybe this wouldn't be so hard after all. But then I saw Wally and his friends coming toward me. *What dumb comment will Wally have for me this time?* I wondered.

But as Wally walked by, he didn't say a thing. Instead, he stuck out his foot and kicked my crutch. I lost my balance and fell to the ground face first.

"Why'd you fall again, Tommy?" he said with a smirk and an evil laugh.

Wally kept walking down the hall, laughing with his friends, and continuing to hurl insults at me as he went. Darn him! Darn these crutches! I could feel my face getting red with anger, but I honestly didn't know how to deal with Wally. Part of me wanted to fight him—crutches or not. I certainly wouldn't mind giving him a knuckle sandwich. Maybe then he would leave me alone.

It would have to wait for another time. I had signatures to get. I picked myself up and headed into the lunchroom.

I went over to Marjorie O'Hara, the smartest person in our class. She was sitting by herself reading a book, as always.

I told her that I was running for president of the student council and asked her to sign my paper. "What's your platform?" Marjorie asked without looking up from her book.

"Um ... My what?"

"Your platform. You've got to have a platform ... you know, some ideas about how you plan to help the school. I can't sign your paper until I know more about your platform."

"But I have to get 50 signatures by Friday, Marjorie," I said.

"So?"

"So I need signatures."

Marjorie looked up at me, straightening her glasses. "Well, you'd better figure out your platform soon, then."

Maybe this wasn't going to be so easy after all.

Marjorie did get me thinking, though. What *was* my platform? What *did* I stand for? I'd have to give it some thought. After all, I'd definitely have to talk about it in my speech.

"I want kids to enjoy school, I want them to have fun activities, and I want kids to be happy at school," I said while walking home with Nicky and Boris.

"That sounds great. Put that in your speech," said Nicky, who was holding the Statue of Liberty he'd made of wood. It was starting to take shape, except now it looked like a man with no arms.

"You have some good ideas, Tommy," said Boris.

Just then I saw Beverly waving from the other side of the street. "I think Beverly wants to talk to you, Tommy," Nicky said.

"Yep. Definitely," Boris agreed.

I hopped across the street and joined Beverly on the sidewalk.

"Hi, Tommy. How are you?" she asked as she tucked her hair behind her ear.

"I'm swell, Beverly. I started getting signatures already. And I'm working on my platform."

"That's great! I'm going to an election rally for FDR tonight with my mother. Would you like to join us?"

Would I ever! "Sure," I said, sounding much calmer out loud than I did in my head.

"Wonderful! Come by my building at six. We can walk there together."

I crossed the street and rejoined Nicky and Boris, but all I could think about was Beverly.

CHAPTER 7

THE RALLY

I met Beverly and her mother outside their apartment building, which was a few streets over from mine. When we got to the rally in the park near the school, I couldn't believe all the people there. It seemed like everyone wanted to hear about this election.

The man in charge of the rally was on stage and speaking into a megaphone. He talked about FDR creating jobs to help farmers and other workers. One woman, who was crying, asked him if he believed things would get better. He paused, then said, "Ma'am, there's as much reason to believe that good things will happen as there are bad. So I choose to believe that good things will happen. And I think FDR feels the same way." People cheered when he announced that FDR would soon be speaking right here in New York City. But I had a problem.

My legs had been hurting me since we arrived at the rally. I did my best to ignore it, but after the rally, as Beverly and I were walking home, they were throbbing.

"Hey Tommy, you're going to let me help you with your speech, right?" Beverly asked.

"Sure," I said, distracted by the pain in my legs.

"Do you want to come over and work on it right now?" she asked. "I'd sure love to get started."

I would really like that too, I thought. *Except not now.* My legs were killing me, and I couldn't concentrate on my speech. But I didn't want Beverly to know I was in pain. "How about another time?" I said. "I'm pretty tired."

It's funny how people can tell when you're not giving them the whole truth. I'm sure she knew that something was fishy. "Sure, another time then," she said. "But would you like to sit on our stoop and talk for a little while? I could bring down some lemonade."

Why did my legs have to hurt now? "Uh, not tonight, Beverly. But thank you. Maybe another time. I'm really beat," I said again.

"OK," Beverly said. I could tell she was trying to hide her disappointment.

"I'm gonna head home now. Goodnight, Beverly."

"Goodnight." As I started to leave, Beverly called out, "Wait, Tommy! Is something wrong?"

I turned back. "Oh no, I'm just really tired," I fibbed. Why couldn't I think of something better to say?

I headed toward my street, relieved that I didn't have to let her see me in pain. But I looked back at her after a few steps and saw that she was staring at the ground. I hoped she wasn't upset. I really liked her and wanted her to like me too.

When I got home I sat on my bed and removed my braces. Then I rubbed my legs. Boy! They sure did hurt. I hadn't been thinking about my legs as much the last couple days, but sitting there on my bed, I started worrying again. Would I ever be able to run and walk without crutches?

And then I remembered what the man said at the rally tonight. There's just as much reason to believe that my legs *will* get better as there is to believe they won't. So why not choose to think positive?

I also thought about how I didn't tell Beverly the truth when she asked me if something was wrong. I felt bad, but I just didn't want to admit to her that I was in pain.

CHAPTER 8

LOST!

The next day at school, I continued getting more signatures. And my legs still hurt.

"Why should I vote for you?" asked Virginia Adams. "Sally Lombardi is running too."

Several kids asked me the same thing, so I said, "I want to make this school great for everyone. I'm still thinking about the best way to do that. But I'd appreciate it if you'd sign this for me anyway. You don't have to vote for me if you don't want to, but I think I'll convince you to ... especially after I give my speech."

Did that just come out of my mouth? It actually sounded pretty good. By the end of the day, I had almost 50 signatures.

After school, I took my paper to the playground with me. It was sunny out, and I was feeling excited about getting the rest of my signatures. Just then I heard, "Hey Polio Legs!" I turned and saw Wally walking toward me.

Not now, I thought. "Leave me alone, Wally. I've got work to do," I muttered.

"What work? What's this?" Wally said as he grabbed for my paper.

"None of your beeswax, Wally! Go play stickball or something, will ya?"

But Wally kept reaching for the paper. I tried to keep it away from him, but he grabbed my arm. Before I knew it, I had fallen down, but I still had the signatures. Wally jumped on top of me, and kept grabbing for my paper. A crowd gathered and cheered me on as Wally and I wrestled on the ground. I tried my best to fight back and still hang on to the paper, but it was no use. Wally pinned me to the ground, tossed my crutches out of reach, and snatched the list of signatures from my hands.

He stood up and read it. Then he said in a nasty way, "*You're* running for student government? I didn't know people with polio legs could do that." I crawled over to my crutches, got back up, and regained my balance.

"Yeah, they can, Wally. All it requires is a brain. Which is why you'd have trouble doing it." I smiled to myself, thinking that I'd given Wally a pretty good comeback. But when I saw his fist coming toward my face, I realized that he was not amused.

He punched me so hard that my whole body twisted around. My crutches went flying again as I fell back and hit the ground. Boy did it hurt! Wally might've been mean and dumber than a box of rocks, but he sure was strong.

"You're lucky you have those crutches, Tommy," he said.

"No, *you're* lucky that I have these crutches, Wally," I said as I rubbed my jaw and wiped a trickle of blood from my nose. We both knew that it wouldn't be so easy to pick on me if I didn't need to use crutches to get around.

Wally just stared at me, processing my threat. Then he did something I didn't expect. I thought he was going to tear my paper into shreds, but instead he placed it on the ground a few feet away from me. I crawled over to get it as quickly as I could, but it was a windy day. Before I knew it, a gust of wind picked up the paper, tossed it over the fence, and blew it across the street. All my signatures were gone.

"Run and get your signatures, Polio Legs!" Wally sneered as he walked away.

But there was nothing I could do.

CHAPTER 9

RUBY'S BIG SURPRISE

"What happened to you, my strong mon?" Ruby asked as I arrived at the hospital for my physical therapy appointment.

"I don't want to talk about it," I grumbled.

"Suit yourself. But we're not going inside today. I have a surprise for you," she said as she led me to a car in the parking lot. A large man dressed in white sat in the driver's seat.

"Where are we going, Ruby? What about physical therapy?"

"Ah, but that *is* where we're going. Now get on in here." So I did.

Ruby's surprise was that she found a pool where I could do my physical therapy exercises—just like FDR! It was in the basement of a place called the Brooklyn-Queens YMCA. And boy, was it huge!

After a while, Ruby came out wearing a full-body bathing suit, a white swim cap on her head, and a bulky life preserver around her shoulders. I'd cleaned the blood off my face and put on a pair of swim trunks that Ruby had brought for me. And I had taken off my braces!

The man who had driven us was already in the pool. His name was Steve, and he was a friend of Ruby's. He was a swim instructor and a lifeguard, so Ruby asked him to help with my water therapy.

"You ready?" Ruby asked.

"I guess so." *Ready as I'll ever be,* I thought.

With that, Ruby and Steve lowered me into the pool. What happened next was the most amazing experience I'd ever had.

As soon as I was in the water, I did something I never thought I'd do again. I walked … without crutches and without braces on my legs! In the water, I could actually walk! Steve held my arms as he moved alongside me. Ruby walked along the edge of the pool cheering me on. For the first time in a long time, I remembered what it was like before I'd gotten polio.

"That's it, my strong mon! You walking now!" she exclaimed.

I walked from one side of the shallow end of the pool to the other and back again. In the water, my legs were able to work because they didn't have to support all of my body weight. After a while I wanted to try it on my own, so I pulled away from Steve and stretched out my arms to help me balance.

I was a little shaky at first, kind of like a newborn colt taking its first steps. But after going back and forth the length of the shallow end a couple of times, I got the hang of it. This was way better than the Pain in the Rump room!

"I think somebody likes this!" Ruby said, her smile stretching across her face.

"Like it? Nah … I *love* it!" I said.

Next, Ruby and I got down to business. Or I should say Steve and I did while Ruby stood by the side of the pool ordering us around. In the water, I was able to do more with my legs than when I did my leg exercises at the hospital. Steve even helped me kick my legs and work on my swimming strokes.

Swimming felt wonderful! Even though I couldn't kick as well as I could before I had polio, I could kick well enough. And my arms did the rest of the work. It was fantastic!

At the end of our session, the three of us sat next to the pool, dangling our feet in the water. Then I remembered something.

"Hey Ruby," I said. "The last few days my legs have been hurting, and I've been worried about it."

"Oh, really?" she said. "Tell me more."

"Well, I've been walking a lot lately, and they just seem to ache more."

"A lot of walking, you say? How much?" she asked.

"I don't know. More than usual," I replied.

"Why?"

"Because I've had things to do and places to go," I said with a laugh.

"And you're worried that your legs are getting worse, I bet?" she said.

"Yeah. Something like that."

"Well, it might be that your leg muscles are getting sore because you're using them more, and they're actually getting stronger."

"What do you mean?" I asked, a little confused.

"See, when you use your muscles, they get sore as they build up strength. And then once they get stronger, they are no longer sore," Ruby explained. "So I'm guessing that your leg muscles are getting stronger and that's why you're feeling some pain."

"Wait! So this is a good thing?" I asked, excited at the idea that my legs might be getting stronger.

"Based on what you're telling me, yes, it's a very good thing. Don't you feel stronger?"

"I guess I do," I admitted.

"And does that pain feel like sore muscles after you've been playing for a long time?"

"Well, now that you mention it, I guess it does."

"I told you, Thomas, you have to believe," Ruby said with a look that said, *You know I'm right.*

After our talk, I got back into the pool and walked and swam until they practically had to drag me out. It felt so good that I didn't want it to end.

"We've got to get you home, Thomas," they kept saying.

But I was too happy to care.

CHAPTER 10

A LESSON
ON BEING POOR

"Extra! Extra! Read all about it!" shouted a boy on the sidewalk while waving a newspaper. "Roosevelt speaking in New York City!"

It was the day after my first water therapy session, and Mom and I were in the breadline again. I was thinking about how I'd lost all my signatures. But seeing so many people waiting in line for food, I started thinking about being poor.

"Are we poor?" I asked my mother while we waited. I figured if we needed to come to the breadline, we must be pretty poor.

"I guess that depends on how you define 'poor,' Thomas," Mom replied. "Can we afford to eat at restaurants and do fun things like go on the rides at Coney Island? No we can't."

"So we *are* poor," I said.

"That doesn't necessarily make us poor," Mom said.

"Huh?" I said, looking at her with a confused look on my face.

"We need money to pay the rent and put food on the table. And, yes, we're struggling to get by. Everybody is. But having money is not more important than having people in your life that you love. It's not as important as doing things that interest you and make you happy, and never giving up hope. Never ever giving up hope."

"Never?" I asked, thinking about how since I got polio I've felt really sad and hopeless sometimes.

"Never, Thomas. Because, no matter what, there's always hope."

We were getting closer to the front of the line and my stomach was growling.

"And if you're grateful for the things you have instead of dwelling on what you don't have, it's really much easier to be happy," Mom continued.

"But I've seen you crying sometimes, Mom," I said.

"That's because I get scared like everyone else. Or sometimes I get really tired, or I just feel like crying. But then I look at you and think about how proud I am of you and how strong and brave you've been dealing with the polio and everything else. I look at the sun shining and I remember all the things I just told you, and then it doesn't seem so bad. Because ... well, because it just isn't. No matter how tough things seem for us right now, they will get better."

"Is that why you and Pop support FDR? Because he didn't give up ... he didn't let having polio stand in his way of running for president?" I asked.

"Yes," she replied. "And because he has good ideas for getting people back to work." She looked at me with a reassuring smile, then closed her eyes and sniffed the air. "Smell that bread?"

I grinned and nodded.

"We're about to eat some of that. Do you feel poor now?"

"Nope," I said. In fact, I felt really lucky to have Mom and Pop and our apartment and my physical therapy sessions with Ruby. I wanted to tell Mom that, but it seemed too mushy, so I just said, "I feel like eating some of that bread."

"Me too," Mom said as she put her arm around me and squeezed my shoulder.

CHAPTER 11

A VICTORY LAP

I arrived at school with a belly full of bread and a renewed sense of hope. I only had two more days to get signatures, but I wasn't going to give up. So what if I had to work a little harder because of Wally's stunt? I wasn't going to let it stop me. I went all around the school and told people that I needed more signatures. And you know what? Everyone was willing to sign my paper again. I worked hard, and by the end of the day, I had the 50 names I needed. I turned them in to the office and was told that I would be on the ballot as a presidential candidate.

I met up with Nicky outside after school and told him the good news. He showed me some posters that he'd drawn. They said, "Vote for Tommy McKnight for School President!" and "Elect Tommy McKnight. He's as good as FDR and better than Hoover!"

"They look fantastic, Nicky! Thanks!" I said as I gave him a pat on the back.

We found Boris outside his family's store and told him the news. He was helping to unload a bunch of fruit from a wagon. When he finished unloading the last box, he looked around, and then looked at me and Nicky. "Hop on, boys," he said. "Quick! Quick!"

"Why?" asked Nicky.

"Don't ask questions. Just hop on!" Boris ordered.

Nicky got in first and then he helped me up. Boris screamed, "Ya! Ya!" as he whipped the reins down on the backs of the two horses attached to the wagon. And off we went!

"It's a victory ride," Boris yelled back at us just as his father came running out of the store shaking his fist and screaming something in Russian.

"What is your father saying?" I asked.

"Just to get back here right away," Boris answered without a hint of fear. "But he'll understand." Who were we to argue?

We flew up and down the neighborhood streets. Kids cheered as they watched us pass. Boris was just wild, yelling out like a cowboy, "Yippie! Yahoo!"

By the time we got back to the store, Boris' entire family was outside—his mother, uncle, aunt, his two older brothers, his brother's wife, and his grandparents. Only his grandfather was smiling.

I thought for sure that we were going to be whipped just like those horses. But amazingly, after Boris said a few words in Russian, the entire family started smiling, shaking my hand, and patting me on the back. "They're congratulating you," Boris said with a grin.

"But I haven't won anything yet," I yelled to Boris.

"They don't know that," he shouted back with a wink.

CHAPTER 12

TOMMY'S BRAIN TRUST

I woke up early on Saturday morning. I kept thinking about how I had to give my speech soon. So after breakfast I sat down to write it. But I really wasn't sure what to say. How do you write a speech?

I looked at the books and magazines I had on FDR and found an article about when he first began his campaign for president. When he decided to run, he put together a group of smart people, including some college professors, to give him advice. They were nicknamed Roosevelt's "brain trust." I decided I'd do the same thing. I would put together a group of people to help me—my very own brain trust.

Nicky and Boris stopped playing outside just to help me write my speech. A guy couldn't ask for better friends. Or, um, a better brain trust. Nicky suggested that we read the speech FDR made when he accepted the Democratic nomination for president—the same one Pop had mentioned. Nicky had listened to it on the radio with his parents, and he thought it might help me write mine. One of the newspapers the librarian, Mrs. Lambeeny, had given me had a copy of the speech. Roosevelt had given the speech in Chicago on July 2 after flying there to accept the nomination. Like my parents said, FDR wanted to show everyone that polio wasn't going to stop him from doing anything.

Boris insisted on reading the speech out loud so I could imagine that I was right there listening to FDR speak. If FDR spoke with a Russian accent, of course. Boris stood on a chair in our kitchen and began.

"Chairman Walsh, my friends of the Democratic National Convention of 1932: ... You have nominated me and ... I am here to thank you for the honor ... "

In the speech, FDR asked:

"What do the people of America want more than anything else? To my mind, they want two things: work ... and a reasonable measure of security ... for themselves and for their wives and children."

He talked about how the government could help get people working again. He mentioned helping farmers and growing forests and how that could improve the economy. He discussed ways to prevent people from losing their homes. It sounded like FDR was really interested in doing anything he could to help. And he had a plan for how to do it.

As Boris continued reading the speech, I heard the words that changed everything for me:

"Out of every crisis, … every disaster, mankind rises with some share of greater knowledge, … of purer purpose."

And then later:

"I pledge you, I pledge myself, to a new deal for the American people… Give me your help, not to win votes alone, but to win in this crusade to restore America to its own people."

"Yeah!" Nicky yelled with enthusiasm. He rose up from his chair, throwing his arms into the air. I cheered and threw my arms up too. But, of course, I couldn't jump out of my seat, and for a moment I felt angry about it.

My eyes filled with tears, and I got a lump in my throat because it felt as if those words had been written just for me. And somewhere inside myself I knew that the man who had written those words sat exactly where I sat. Angry, frustrated, and stuck in a chair because his legs didn't work right. I realized then that FDR wasn't just speaking about people being poor, he was speaking about having polio, just like me. And what he was saying was that I *will* be better because of this—because of having polio. And right then and there, I knew he was right. Now I just had to figure out how to get this into my speech.

After meeting with my brain trust, I sat down and started writing. Beverly had offered to help me, but I hadn't talked to her since the rally, and I didn't know how to explain why I acted the way I did. Besides, I felt this was something I needed to do on my own.

I wrote that having polio taught me about courage, friendship, and people helping each other. I wrote that it taught me about hard work and patience. I said that I wanted to make school a fun place to learn things. I even promised that I'd fight for less homework on weekends. Within an hour I had a full page and over the next couple days I'd pretty much finished it.

∞

I went to the pool again with Ruby and Steve twice that week. After doing all kinds of exercises, I even swam a few laps. I was able to kick my legs even better than the last time.

On the walk home I practiced my speech:

"Good morning, Principal Rogers and my fellow classmates. Thank you for giving me this opportunity to tell you why I'd like to be class president.

Most of you know that I had polio, and as you can see, I'm not the same boy that I was two years ago. Sure, polio left me without the use of my legs, which is no fun. Believe me. But it has also taught me a lot. It's taught me about courage, hard work, and patience.

Franklin Delano Roosevelt had polio too. But he didn't let it stop him from running for president, and I won't either. I may not be able to run and jump like the rest of you anymore, but I have a lot of ideas for how to make school more fun. First, I plan to … "

It was pretty good. But then I started thinking about Beverly again. I had written the speech without her, and I felt bad about it. I knew she wanted to help. I wondered what she was up to.

I decided to go over to her apartment. I was hoping she'd be outside playing, but she wasn't. I thought about ringing the bell, but I didn't. FDR's speech in town was coming up, so I left a note on her door asking if she still wanted to go together.

I was starting to feel pretty good about my speech, but I was still nervous about standing in front of the whole school. What if I tripped? What if someone made fun of me? Or what if Wally yelled out "Polio Legs" or something mean like that? I believed in what I was saying, and if people were going to be mean, I wasn't going to let it stop me. I kept telling myself that, but that didn't stop the butterflies from flitting around in my stomach.

CHAPTER 13

A BIG MAN AND A LITTLE BOY

I didn't see Beverly at school before FDR's speech, so I wasn't sure if she'd gotten my note. I decided to stop by her place on my way to the speech. I told my parents I would meet them there. There was no answer when I rang the bell at Beverly's house.

I got to the assembly hall just before FDR took the stage. The auditorium was completely packed. I tried to find Beverly and my parents, but there were so many people crowded into the room, it was impossible. FDR's voice boomed over the speakers:

> "... every one of our people is entitled to the opportunity to earn a living ... These hopes, these ambitions, have struggled for realization in different ways, on the farms, in the cities, in the factories, among businessmen and in the homes."

I could hear him clearly, but I couldn't see very well. I wanted to get closer, so I tried to squeeze through the mob of people and make my way toward the front.

"Move it, kid," one man growled as he nudged me.

"Hey! Watch it!" grumbled another, whose foot I accidentally bumped with my crutch.

But then a nice man said, "Coming through!" and people moved out of the way so I could get closer. Slowly, I made it through the crowd until I got to the front.

Roosevelt was magnificent! He stood in the middle of the stage at a podium that was draped with an American flag. He wore a black suit with a vest and a white flower pinned to his jacket. He looked very dapper! He looked like a president. His voice was smooth and powerful as he spoke into the microphone in front of him.

"There is among you the man who has been brought up in the good American tradition to work hard and to save for a rainy day. You have worked hard," Roosevelt continued. *"You now find your savings gone. You now find your job gone."*

I scanned the audience, looking around for Beverly or my parents. I didn't see them, but I noticed that everyone in the crowd was fascinated by FDR. They hung on his every word, grateful for what he was saying and wanting to believe that he could make a difference in their lives.

> *"We have not enticed you with offers of magic, or lured you with vain promises … We have pledged you our word and our will to do,"* Roosevelt assured the crowd.

And then, across the floor, right in front of FDR but on the other side of the room, I saw a little boy. Just like me, he wore crutches on his arms and braces on his legs. Polio legs. He couldn't have been more than 6 or 7 years old, and I wondered if he even understood what FDR was saying. He was standing next to a large man in dirty pants and work boots. The man placed one hand on the boy's arm to help him balance. The boy had tears rolling down his cheeks as he listened to FDR.

I couldn't take my eyes off the little boy, and he couldn't take his eyes off FDR. I stood there watching him with his father. The boy's bright, smiling face was filled with hope. And I understood why.

After the speech, I found my parents. As we walked home together, I thought about Beverly. With all the people there, I must have missed her. *I sure hope she doesn't think that I don't like her anymore,* I thought. I'd explain it to her at school on Monday.

Monday. The day of my speech. Yikes! I was still nervous, but after seeing FDR, I was ready. People were interested in what he had to say. And no one seemed to care a lick about his polio.

CHAPTER 14

SHOWTIME

On Monday morning, Mom helped me get dressed in a crisp white shirt. Then she pulled out a suit jacket.

"Where'd that come from, Mom?"

"I made it from one of your father's old suit jackets," she said.

"But he's so big!"

"Well, it took a lot of sewing," she giggled.

When I tried it on, it fit like a glove. Pop thought so too. He helped me put on one of his ties, and soon I was off to school.

Nicky was waiting for me outside. When we got to school, we saw Boris walking down the hall toward us.

"Oh no," he said, when he saw me.

"Doesn't Tommy look dapper?" Nicky said.

"Yeah, he looks swell," Boris replied. "But we have a problem."

"What's the problem?" I asked with a sinking feeling in my stomach.

"You need a flower," Boris said with a grin.

"A *flower*?" I asked, a bit confused.

"Yes. FDR wears a flower on his coat. I'll go find you one." And just like that Boris was running down the hall and out the door.

Nicky reached into his pocket and pulled out his Statue of Liberty carving. It actually looked pretty good now. "I want you to have this," he said. "For good luck."

"Thanks, Nicky," I said as I looked at his handiwork. "You're a good friend."

Boris came storming down the hall, out of breath. He skidded to a stop right in front of us. He had a big white flower in his hand.

"Here you go … Just like FDR," Boris said as he stuck the flower in the lapel of my jacket. "Now you're all set!"

"Yep! You're ready, Tommy," Nicky said. "Now go get 'em!"

The entire school was gathered in the gymnasium. The posters that Nicky had made for my campaign lined the walls, as did posters for Sally Lombardi, Joel Morganstern, and candidates for the other offices.

I waited outside in the hallway until it was my turn to speak. I heard lots of clapping and laughing coming from inside the gymnasium as the other candidates gave their speeches. My heart was racing, my palms were clammy, and my stomach was doing backflips. I was nervous but excited at the same time.

Then the door opened and Boris peeked his head out. "You're up, Tommy," he said.

As I moved to the podium, the room became silent—so silent I could hear my braces squeaking and my heart pounding. I set my crutches against the podium, took my speech out of my pocket, and spread it out in front of me. Then I took a deep breath and looked up. All eyes were on me. There was Larry Prescott, Virginia Adams, and Marjorie O'Hara. And there was Beverly. She gave me a comforting smile that said, "You can do this!" That helped me relax a bit. I smiled back and looked down at my speech.

I was just about to start when I heard: "Hey, Polio Legs!" Wally's voice echoed across the silent gym. A few people giggled and everyone turned to look at him. *Oh no! Not now!* I thought.

"How's your polio legs?" Wally and his big mouth shouted before I could even get started.

I took another deep breath and then said into the microphone, "Uh … Hello, my name is Tommy McKnight. And since Wally is asking, my polio legs are fine." The students roared with laughter.

Wally's wisecrack had left me so flustered that I lost my place in my notes. I had no choice but to wing it for a while until I could get back on track.

"In fact, I'm getting stronger every day. And just like FDR, I won't ever let it stop me!" A few students clapped and cheered.

"I may not be able to run and jump like the rest of you anymore, but I have a lot of ideas for how to make this school more fun. Are you ready to hear how I plan to do that?" I asked.

"Yeah!" shouted Larry Prescott. And then I heard a few more "yeahs" in agreement.

So much for Wally trying to ruin my speech, I thought. The audience was ready to listen to what I had to say.

"What do the students of McKinley Junior High School want more than anything else? To my mind, they want two things: less homework and more fun activities while we're at school. I pledge you, I pledge myself, to a new deal for the students of McKinley Junior High!"

I continued by stating some of my ideas for how I was going to make those things happen. When I looked to the side of the stage for just a second, I saw Boris leaning against the wall. He had his arms crossed and his head held high. He looked right at me, gave me a thumbs-up, and nodded his head as if to say, "You're doing great!" And I was.

"Hi Tommy! Your speech was terrific!" Beverly said in the gym after the assembly was over.

"Thanks, Beverly!" I said.

"I'm going to vote for you," she whispered. "I think a lot of people will."

"Really?" I asked.

"Yes. You were funny and your ideas were really smart," she replied. "And the way you handled Wally ... Boy, you really put him in his place!"

"I'm sorry you didn't get to help with my speech," I said.

"That's OK."

"Listen Beverly. I was worried that I hurt your feelings the other night after the rally. I'm sorry that I left so fast."

"It's OK. You were tired."

"I was sort of tired, but the truth is that my legs really hurt, and I didn't want you to think there was something wrong with me or that I'm not strong."

"Oh, Tommy! I've never thought for a second that there was anything wrong with you. And I think you are very strong."

"Really?" I asked.

"Really. I like you just the way you are, Tommy."

In the books and movies they always talk about falling in love. I never really knew what that meant. Love was for grown-ups. But right then I felt something warm and squishy in my chest. Was it love? I don't know. What I did know is that, at that moment, I liked Beverly even more than I ever had.

CHAPTER 15

TROUBLE AT THE BEACH

When the speeches were finished, we took a class field trip to Brighton Beach. After a picnic lunch, we could play games, go swimming, and take boat rides. Nicky, Boris, and I took a boat ride, and then headed to the swimming area.

I took off my braces, and Nicky and Boris helped me get into the water. I felt so strong in the water—like I could do anything! Most of the other kids were swimming too—except for Wally. He was sitting off by himself and wouldn't go into the water.

It was a fun afternoon, but around 3:00 p.m., the lifeguards ordered us out of the water. We were all getting dressed, gathering our things, and getting ready to go home.

That's when I saw Wally sneak off and go into the water. *What on earth is he doing?* I thought. *He sits on the beach all day, and when the lifeguards tell us to get out of the water, then he decides to go swimming!*

He started swimming away from one of the piers, but soon, I could tell he was having trouble. The waves were choppy, and Wally's head kept going underwater.

I was sitting on the edge of another pier getting dressed, and nobody else was nearby. Without a second thought, I grabbed two life preservers, plunged into the water, and began swimming out to Wally. By the time I got to him, I could see he was really struggling. He was bobbing up and down in the water and gasping for air. When he saw me, his head dipped underwater. I threw a life preserver over his neck and helped him swim back to the shore.

When we got there, Wally was coughing and trying to catch his breath. Finally, after what seemed like forever, he looked over at me. "Um ... Thanks, Tommy. I ... um ... well, thanks," was all he managed to say.

"Why did you do that?" I screamed.

"Because all day I watched everyone else swimming and having so much fun and, well ... "

"You can't swim, can you?" I asked.

"No ... I never learned how," he said, bowing his head in embarrassment.

"Then why did you try ... especially with no lifeguards around?"

"Because I didn't want anyone to know that I can't swim. I'm the best athlete in school, Tommy. What would everyone think if they knew I couldn't swim?"

Wally coughed a couple more times, and I could tell he was feeling pretty lousy. "Thanks for helping me," he said again. "I'm sorry for calling you Polio Legs and all that stuff."

I wanted to ask Wally why he did and said all those mean things to me. But at the moment, I kind of felt sorry for him. "It's fine, Wally. Let's just forget about it."

For a few moments, we sat there on the beach in silence, neither of us knowing what to say or do next. "Hey, don't tell anyone about this, OK?"

"OK, Wally," I said.

"So, is it all right if I vote for you?" Wally asked.

"Sure, Wally. That would be swell!"

Just then, Nicky and Boris came by with my braces and crutches. "What's going on?" Boris asked.

"Nothing," I said as I put my braces on. "We're just clearing the air."

Just then I had an idea. I turned to Wally and said, "By the way, I know a great swim instructor if you really want to learn how to swim."

CHAPTER 16

DO YOU BELIEVE?

"Run, Tommy! Run!" they screamed. Faster and faster I sprinted. And soon I was running so fast that I lifted into the air and was flying high up in the clouds. I heard street trolleys and the kerplunk, kerplunk *of horse's hooves on the street below. As I soared higher and higher, it felt so good to be free. And when I got to the highest cloud, I laid down on it. It was soft and fluffy and white. I just lay there and enjoyed myself …*

And then I woke up.

After school I got to the hospital just as Ruby was finishing up with another patient. When she saw me, she turned, smiled that big, bright smile and said, "There's my strong mon. How strong are ya today, my strong mon? Stronger than yesterday I bet. Ha ha ha."

I told Ruby about my speech while I did my exercises. She was really happy for me. When we were all finished, she said, "You lookin' a lot stronger these days, Thomas, a lot stronger."

"I feel stronger, Ruby," I said.

Then I thought about how much Ruby had helped me, and I felt so lucky and grateful. "I really want to thank you for all the ways you've helped me, Ruby," I said as I gave her a big hug.

"You did all the hard work, Thomas," she said.

"Yeah, but you've helped me do things I didn't think I could," I replied.

"Wasn't me that helped you," she said as she grinned and rubbed her hands together. "Was my magic. I told ya that. All I did was work my magic. And I think somewhere along the way, you started to believe," she said. Then she leaned down and looked me in the eye. "You *do* believe, don't ya, Thomas?"

The truth was, I did believe. I believed that things could get better. I believed that even if I was having trouble with my legs or anything in life, I would still be OK—better than OK.

I believed that if I worked hard and stayed positive, good things would happen. And I guess maybe I believed in magic a little too.

I looked into Ruby's eyes, smiled back at her, and said, "I do."

∞

Walking home from the hospital, I was thinking about Ruby and magic and staying positive. I was lost in thought until I heard the song "Happy Days Are Here Again," playing from a radio in someone's apartment. I hummed along with it until I couldn't hear it anymore.

You never know what good things are waiting for you around the next corner, I thought to myself as I turned onto my street. As for the bad things—let 'em come. I've got my family, my friends, and most important of all, I've got myself. And I like myself. Turns out happy days are here again ... even for me. Go figure!

EPILOGUE

On November 7, 1932, Tommy McKnight won the McKinley Junior High School election for seventh grade class president. The next day, Franklin Delano Roosevelt won the presidential election. He beat Herbert Hoover in a landslide to become the 32nd president of the United States.

ABOUT THE AUTHOR

Danny Kravitz is an Emmy-award-winning writer and songwriter and a professor of screenwriting at Columbia College in Chicago. He has written for TV, film, and print media. Danny combines his passion for storytelling with his love of history. He is also a sports and nature enthusiast. He resides in Chicago.

MAKING CONNECTIONS

1. What is the theme of this story? What details from the story support the theme?

2. Tommy, the main character of this novel, had polio. What is polio, and how has it affected Tommy's lifestyle?

3. Describe either Tommy or Wally, and explain how the character changes throughout the novel.

4. How does Franklin Delano Roosevelt inspire Tommy? Use evidence from the text to support your answer.

5. Describe the setting for this novel. In what ways would the story have been different if it was set in the present day? How would it be the same?

6. Use examples from the text to compare and contrast Tommy and Wally. How are the boys alike? How are they different?

GLOSSARY

assembly (uh-SEM-blee)—a meeting of lots of people

ballot (BAL-uht)—a piece of paper, or a card, used to vote in an election

breadline (BRED-lyn)—a line of people who are waiting to receive free food

campaign (kam-PAYN)—a series of organized actions and events with a specific goal, such as being elected

dapper (DAP-ur)—neat or stylish in dress or appearance

Democratic National Convention (de-muh-KRA-tik NASH-uh-nuhl kuhn-VEN-shuhn)—a large meeting during which a political party chooses its candidates

embarrass (em-BAR-uhs)—to feel self-conscious or ashamed or to cause someone else to feel that way

enthusiasm (en-THOO-zee-az-uhm)—great excitement or interest

flit (FLIT)—to move or fly quickly from one place or thing to another

flustered (FLUHS-turd)—nervous or confused

frustrated (FRUHS-trate-ed)—discouraged or upset about something

galumph (guh-LUMF)—to move in a loud, clumsy way

governor (GUHV-ur-nur)—a person elected to be the head of a state's government

Great Depression (GRAYT di-PRESH-uhn)—a period of hard times from 1929 to 1939 in the United States when many people lost their jobs and had little money or food

hobble (HAH-buhl)—to walk with difficulty because of injury or weakness

instinctive (in-STINGK-tiv)—something that comes naturally without thinking about it

Model T (MOD-uhl TEE)—a car made by the Ford Motor Company from 1908 to 1927; it was regarded as one of the first affordable cars in the United States

nomination (nah-muh-NAY-shun)—the choice of a person to run for a political office

palooka (puh-LOO-kuh)—an inexperienced or incompetent boxer; a slang term for someone who is clumsy or stupid

persecution (pur-suh-KYOO-shuhn)—cruel or unfair treatment, often because of race or religious beliefs

podium (POH-dee-uhm)—a raised platform for a speaker or performer

polio (POH-lee-oh)—a disease that attacks the nerves, spinal cord, and brain

rally (RAL-ee)—a meeting of a large group of people to create excitement about a common interest

sarcasm (SAHR-kaz-uhm)—a remark usually made to hurt someone's feelings or show scorn

sensation (sen-SAY-shuhn)—a feeling that the body experiences

trolley (TRAH-lee)—an electric streetcar that runs on tracks and gets power from an overhead wire

STRAIGHT FROM HISTORY

The Great Depression
(1929–1939)

After World War I, businesses were booming. The decade that followed was known as "The Roaring Twenties" because a lot of people were earning more money than ever before. Many invested their money in the stock market in hopes of making a fortune. But "The Roaring Twenties" came to an end when the stock market crashed on October 29, 1929. Many people lost their life savings and their jobs. By 1933, almost half of all U.S. banks had gone out of business, and nearly 15 million people were out of work. President Franklin Roosevelt's New Deal programs put many people back to work in the 1930s. But the U.S. economy did not fully recover until 1939 when World War II began and American industries ramped up production for the war effort.

Herbert Hoover
(1874–1964)

Herbert Hoover is often remembered as the president who was unable to get the United States out of the Great Depression. But he had many successes before his time as president (1929–1933). During World War I (1914–1918) Hoover organized efforts to conserve food and supplies needed for the war effort. After the war, President Wilson put Hoover in charge of getting food, clothing, and other supplies to Europe, where many homes and factories had been destroyed. His efforts brought 34 million tons of food and supplies to people in 20 countries.

Franklin Delano Roosevelt
(1882–1945)

Elected to four terms in office, Franklin Delano Roosevelt was America's longest-serving president (1933–1945). A powerful and popular leader, he led the nation out of the Great Depression and through World War II. While on vacation in 1921, Roosevelt contracted polio. The crippling disease left him unable to use his legs. However, many Americans were unaware that Roosevelt couldn't walk because the press was not allowed to show him in a wheelchair. He even appeared to walk when he accepted the Democratic nomination for president in 1932. In reality, he let go of his son's arm, grabbed the podium, and used a cane to scoot his legs forward. He died a few months into his fourth term. Soon after, World War II ended.

Polio

Polio is a disease that spreads from contact with a person infected with the poliovirus. It mainly affects children, but some adults, such as Franklin Roosevelt, contract the virus too. Some of those infected with the poliovirus have flulike symptoms that go away after a few days. In rare cases, the poliovirus can affect the brain and spinal cord and can lead to paralysis (the inability to move or feel parts of the body) and even death. By the early 1950s, polio caused about 3,000 deaths and 15,000 cases of paralysis each year. By 1955, a vaccine was available thanks to the research of scientist Jonas Salk. Today, children are typically vaccinated by age 6. As a result, no cases of polio have developed in the United States since 1979. Efforts are under way to wipe out the disease worldwide.

Read more about
U.S. presidential elections
and politics with

CONNECT

Or discover great websites and books like this
one at **www.facthound.com**. Just type in the
book **ID: 9781496525857** and you're ready to go.